NEW CAT

Yangsook Choi

Frances Foster Books

Farrar, Straus and Giroux ● New York

Distributed in Canada by Douglas & McIntyre Ltd.
Color separations by Hong Kong Scanner Arts
Printed and bound in the United States of America by Berryville Graphics
Designed by Judith M. Lanfredi
First edition, 1999

Library of Congress Cataloging-in-Publication Data
Choi, Yangsook.
    New cat / Yangsook Choi. — 1st ed.
        p.   cm.
    Summary: Shortly after coming to America, Mr. Kim, owner of
a tofu factory in the Bronx, gets a fluffy silver cat that makes her
home in his factory and one night saves it from burning down.
    ISBN 0-374-35512-6
    [1. Cats—Fiction. 2. Korean Americans—Fiction.]   I. Title.
PZ7.C446263Ne 1998
[E]—dc21   97-15668

To my parents

New Cat lived in a tofu factory in the Bronx in New York City.

At four o'clock every morning, Mr. Kim, the owner of the factory, arrived at his office to start the day. "Good morning," he would call as he stepped through the front door.

"*Mi-yao!*" New Cat would answer.

They were best friends.

Mr. Kim had found New Cat at an animal shelter when he'd first come to America from Korea. He had needed a friend as much as she had. She was smaller than a tofu block then.

When he brought her to work, people said, "Oh, you got a new cat!"

"Yes, New Cat!" Mr. Kim exclaimed with pride.

That's how New Cat got her name.

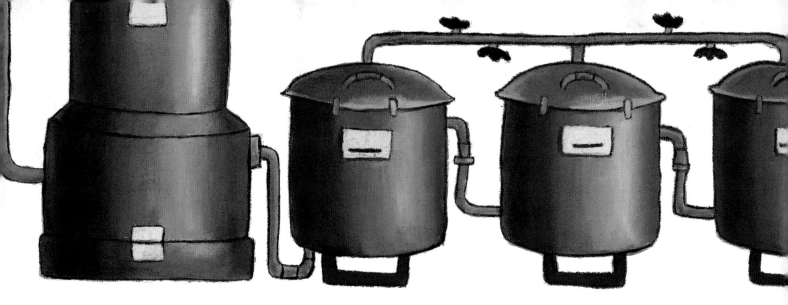

New Cat watched Mr. Kim work hard to make the best tofu in all of New York City. New Cat worked hard, too. It was her job to hold down the paper while Mr. Kim was writing, clean the computer monitor with her tail, and taste the tofu for Mr. Kim when he put it in her bowl. But her most important job was to keep mice out of the factory.

New Cat loved everything about living in the tofu factory except for one thing. She had seen a mouse in the production room and Mr. Kim didn't allow New Cat to go in there. How could New Cat do her job properly if she couldn't get out to chase the mouse?

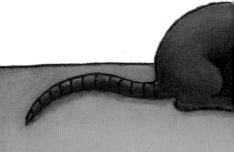

One quiet night, New Cat was awakened by a scratching sound. She opened her eyes and there was the mouse, right in front of her nose. New Cat waited for just the right moment, then sprang. But the mouse was too fast. It escaped under the door into the production room.

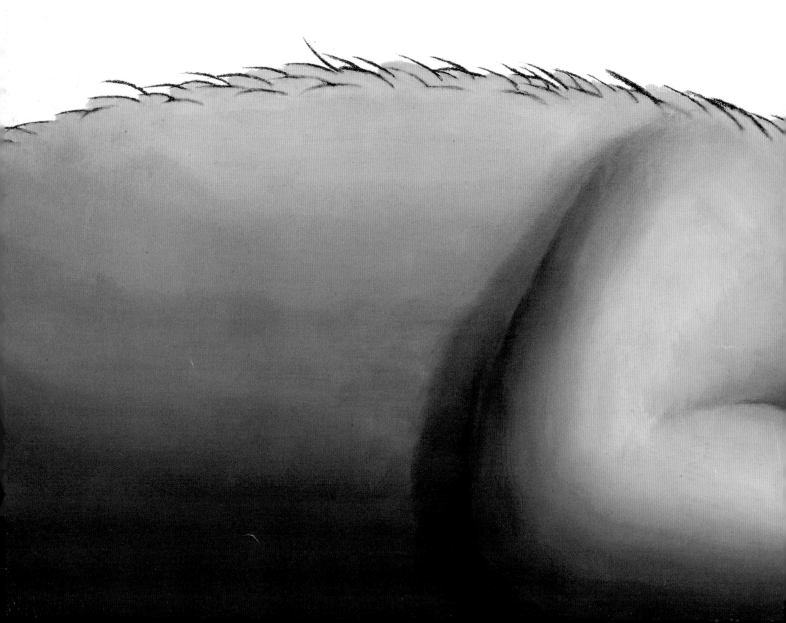

New Cat scratched at the production-room door and found that it wasn't tightly closed. She wasn't supposed to go in there, but she also knew that the mouse was up to no good. She didn't know what to do.

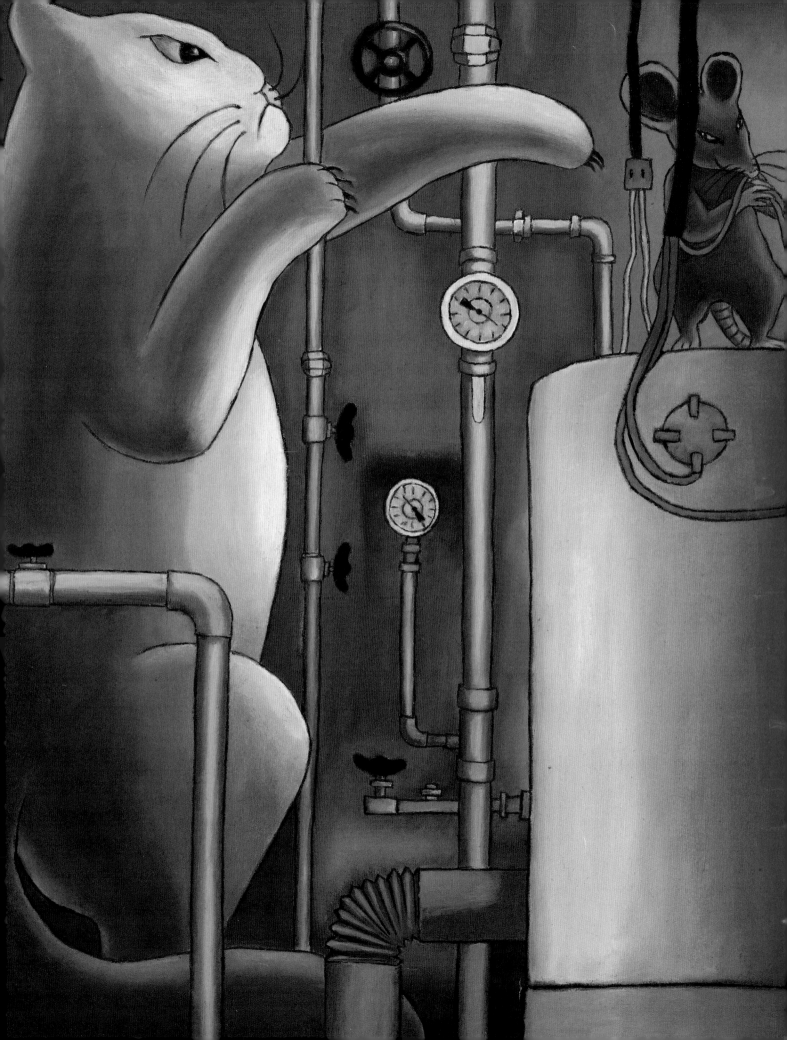

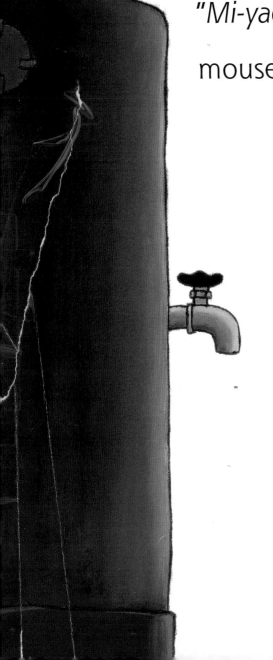

With her ears pricked backward and her tail twitching, New Cat slipped through the door into the production room. She spotted the mouse right away, standing on top of a water boiler. It was chewing the electric wires. "*Mi-yao.*" New Cat pounced, but the mouse was too fast and got away.

Then New Cat saw something strange.

A bright orange light waved in the corner.

It grew bigger and bigger and then lunged

toward New Cat. It was hot!

Smoke filled the air. There was a terrible noise
of screaming sirens.

New Cat tried to go back to Mr. Kim's office,
but the hot orange light blocked her path.
She ran the other way and leaped onto a
cart loaded with a bucket full of tofu.

Firefighters broke through the factory door and aimed their hoses at the fire. By the time Mr. Kim arrived, the fire was almost out.

"I must thank you for saving my factory," he said to the firefighters.

"Actually, the fire couldn't get past that big pile of tofu on the floor," said one of the firefighters. "That's what kept the fire from spreading before we got here. You're lucky it was there."

"Oh," said Mr. Kim. "That makes sense. Tofu is mostly water."

But he wondered how the tofu had spilled.

While the firefighters got ready to leave, Mr. Kim headed for his office to check on New Cat. But the office door stood open and New Cat was not there.

"New Cat! New Cat!" he called. He waited for the familiar *"Mi-yao,"* but New Cat didn't answer.

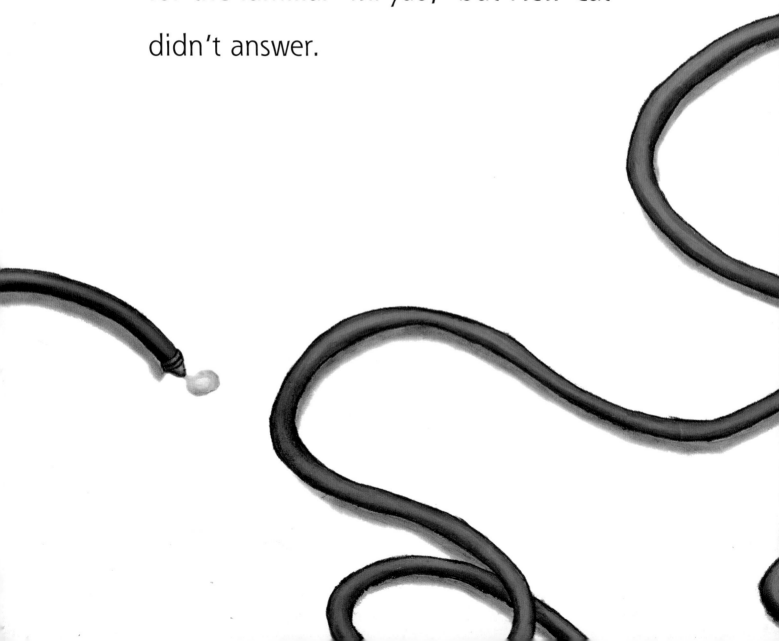

"She's been my best friend for seven years, ever since I came to America," Mr. Kim said sadly.

A firefighter put his hand on Mr. Kim's shoulder. "Don't worry," he said. "Your cat probably just got scared and ran away. She'll turn up when she knows the danger has passed. Go on home and get some sleep."

But Mr. Kim knew he wouldn't be able to sleep. He was too worried about New Cat.

After the firemen had left, Mr. Kim decided
to clean up the spilled tofu.
Suddenly a bucket of tofu began to shake.
"*Mi-yao*," it said. And out of the bucket
climbed a very wet cat.

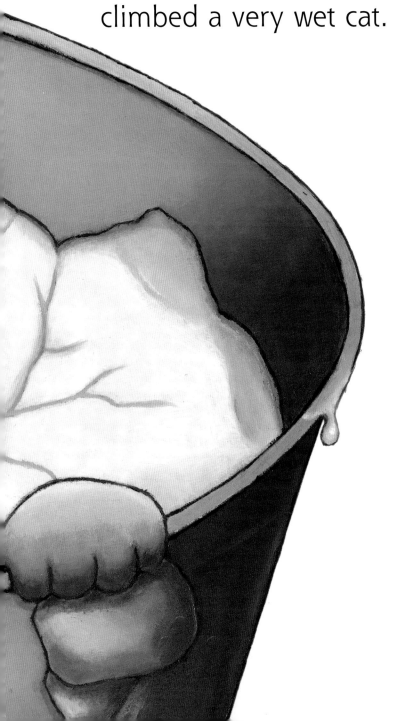

Mr. Kim was delighted. "Oh, New Cat!" he said. "I was so worried about you!"

"*Mi-yao*," New Cat answered, as if nothing had happened.

The next day, Mr. Kim fixed the door so mice could never get into the production room again. New Cat was very happy to go back to her office life, where she could watch to make sure that Mr. Kim was still making the very best tofu in all of New York City.

"Fresh tofu! Fresh tofu!"

This cry, coming up from the street, used to wake me early every morning when I was a little girl in Korea. The tofu vendor walked along, carrying his wooden box full of tofu on his shoulder. My mother would always buy some, and the tofu would appear in a hot stew, or in a crispy pan-fried meat dish with vegetables, or sometimes in a thick, spicy red sauce. My mother told me that tofu was made from dried soybeans, which were soaked, drained, and ground. She said that eating tofu would make me healthy and give me beautiful skin.

Tofu has been my favorite food ever since, even after I moved to New York City. One day I was eating tofu for lunch and the thought of writing about it came to me. I visited a tofu factory to learn more about how tofu is made, and left with a bucketful of tofu to inspire me.

Enjoy your tofu!